Cat I

FINDING YOUR DREAM

Cat Detectives Little One and Captain Spunky and The Humane Society of the United States share a common goal: to protect and care for animals...no matter how big, no matter how small. Join us in your support as we strive to better the life of homeless animals. If you're looking for a pet, go to your local animal shelter and adopt one today! If you can't have your own pet, support The Humane Society of the United States.

Also, the Cat Detectives want to thank the Humane Society of the United States for helping the writer of this book by sharing their thoughts and ideas and providing insight about the caring people who work in animal shelters throughout the United States. And on a personal note, I, Captain Spunky wouldn't be where I am without the help of the people at an animal shelter.

Aloha Publications
www.catdetectives.com

To Kristen -
Happy thoughts
and dreams!
Darla Zuhoeu (Boyd)
10-06-01

i

Available soon!

A continuation of your favorite series with famous Cat Detectives Little One and Captain Spunky!

Tale of Three Amigos

Tale of an Egyptian Princess

Tale of a Hollywood Superstar

Tale of the Wild West

A South Sea Adventure

Stranded on Cat Island

Who Says There's No Easter Bunny?

A Tale of a New Yorkie

Available now at a bookstore near you:
Tale of a Christmas Angel

"I loved the cats. This book was awesome. I thought that Priscilla the butterfly was so cool. I couldn't wait each night for my Mom to read it to me. I could see all the neat things happening."

Abbey Williams, age 8

"This was a very good story. It made me sad, it made me happy. I really liked the happy ending. Spunky was my favorite character. If you like cats as much as I do, then you'll love this book. I can't wait for the next one!"

Emily Dunaway, age 9

"Captain Spunky's journey from lonely kitten to beloved member of a family left us with the desire to rescue a Captain Spunky of our own. This book was a joy to read and an inspiration to animal lovers of any age."

The Earley family, Tyler age 13, Ryan age 8, and Austin age 3

'**Finding your Dream**' is an animal lover's book — of any age. Once you start it, you won't want to put it down."

Cat Detectives of America Club

"In **Finding your Dream,** Darla Zuhdi's new book in the Cat Detectives' series, Baby Spunky realizes his dream of having a loving family and home, but he finds it only after several suspense-filled adventures."

Shelley Howe Rutherford, Ed.D.

"Parents everywhere can breathe a sigh of relief and trust even their youngest children with these frisky felines. Get set for another rollicking adventure with the fearless Cat Detectives."

Hazel Reyes, Missionary

Reviews for Tale of a Christmas Angel

"highly recommended...a Christmas must have."
KKVV Christian radio, Las Vegas, Nevada

"...a cat lover's delight..."
The Sunday Oklahoman

"delightful" and "...couldn't put it down."
OETA, public television

GuideLive recommendation
Dallas Morning News, Sunday edition

Dedicated to the "four grandmothers,"
grandmothers everywhere, and
"Uncle" Rich Barker
God bless you all!

And, as always, special thanks to my
husband Bill,
my entire family, and my nephew who was
the inspiration
for the character, Stevie

FINDING YOUR DREAM

ISBN No.: 0-9706062-1-4

Printed in the United States of America
First Printing
Cover and interior art by Marietta Egervary and Leslie Walulek of Emerson Egervary & Associates, Inc. Mechanicsburg, PA
Edited by Shelley Rowe Rutherford, Ed.D.
Aloha Publications Paperbacks edition/May 2001
10 9 8 7 6 5 4 3 2 1

Finding your Dream

Darla Zuhdi

---
an
Aloha Publication
Paperback

Aloha Publications
Hawaii

My friend

Snuggled up beside my feet
my furry friend does sleep;
tired from his escapades
he doesn't stir a peep.

But when I look down to see
if my pal is awake,
he stretches his little paw
as if he wants to shake.

Smiling, I grasp his foot
and give a gentle tug;
then onto my lap he leaps
for a kiss, pet, and hug.

Darla Zuhdi

Prologue

"You got it: we'll solve it," Captain Spunky said, looking at Little One hopefully.

She giggled. "They won't know what it means, silly. How about, you got a mystery, we'll make it history. That's a good slogan, don't you think?"

Stripe, a silver and white cat that lived up the street, jumped up and down with enthusiasm. "Ooooh! I like that one."

"Yeah. That was really good," Captain Spunky agreed.

He looked at Little One and silently appraised her. She was beautiful. She had pretty blue almond-shaped eyes and her rich, dark brown face, legs, and tail contrasted nicely with her sandy colored coat.

He shook his head slowly. There was no way anyone would guess that inside that pretty little head of hers, she was the best cat detective in the business. Well, the best detective until he had come along.

For three years, he'd been watching and learning as Little One solved cases and mysteries. During that time, she had taught him so much about being a detective, he was sure he could make her proud.

In fact, the little party that was being thrown on that date was in honor of his induction into the CDA, the Cat Detectives of America. Last month, Little One had nominated him to be included in the club. And yesterday, they'd found out his nomination was accepted.
It was official. He was a detective.

Captain Spunky surveyed the group of cats gathered around him with pride. These were his friends. He could count on them through thick and thin, better or worse, through good times and bad.

But it hadn't always been like that. As a kitten, he'd had to fight to survive. Forced to find food where he could and homeless, his future was bleak.

Then one day.....

Chapter One
Voyage to a Destiny

It had been a day and half since the humans had abandoned the three pint-sized black kittens in a field, trapped in a large cardboard box. Since then, they'd been patiently waiting for the humans to come back and bring them food. But they hadn't, and as time went by, they were getting hungrier and hungrier.

And grumpier and grumpier.

Trixie, the smallest of the kittens, struggled to stand as an uncontrollable shiver attacked her tiny body. "I'm cold," she wailed.

"I am too, Trixie," her sister Powderpuff replied. She looked at her brother with wide eyes. "Do you think they're coming back?"

Spunky, the strongest of the three kittens, stood up to face them. "I don't know. All I know is that I'm cold and I'm hungry and I'm tired of being stuck in this box."

"We've got to wait for them," Trixie whimpered.

"We don't even know if they will be back. What

we've got to do is get some food or we're going to — "

"Don't say it," Powderpuff interrupted him. "We're going to be fine."

"We're not going to be if we continue to sit around in here and do nothing," he said stubbornly. "They've been gone for a day and a half. I don't think they're coming back." He lifted his chin. "I'm the man of the family and it's my job to take care of you. I say it's time to go."

Neither of his sisters moved.

He leaned over to grip Powderpuff's tail in his mouth and pulled. "Come on!" he told her firmly. "I'm not kidding." He glanced at Trixie and lowered his voice so his sickly sister couldn't hear him. "She's not getting any better. If we don't get some food in her, she's not going to make it."

Powderpuff swiped her small egg-shaped paw across her runny nose and sniffled. "I'm scared," she admitted. "I don't know where we are and there are big things out there."

He smiled briefly at her. "Powderpuff, we're so small those big things won't even see us."

She looked at him hesitantly, only partially convinced by his words. "You think so?"

"I know so," he said with more confidence than he really felt. Actually, he was scared, too, but he knew he had to act as if he weren't. He glanced over at her. "If you and I lean on the side of this box at the same time, I think we can tip it over."

"O — kay," she answered skeptically. "I hope you know what you're doing."

"Trust me." He flicked his long, fluffy tail and at the same time puffed out his itty-bitty chest.

3

She looked at him and grinned. Spunky was the only kitten of the litter that had white tufts of hair under his chin. Every other part of him was black. The white fur made him look as if he had a white bow tie around his neck, as if he were ready at a moment's notice to go to a party, dressed in his finest.

Powderpuff knew that if her brother was aware how handsome he was, he'd be very hard to live with. But as it was, she could handle him just fine. She was a much better wrestler and any time he got out of line, she'd just pin him to the ground.

After several frustrating minutes, the two tiny kittens realized they were going to have trouble getting out of the box. They'd already tried to stand on their hind legs and lean against the cardboard wall at the same time. Yet try as they might, they couldn't get the box to tip over.

"What are we going to do?" Powderpuff moaned.

"I don't know," he answered as he sat down and scratched his ear. Boy oh boy was he itchy. He wanted to scratch all over. If only he could get on some grass and wiggle his body around, then he was sure the itchiness would go away. He looked around the box. He had to do something to fix the jam they were in. They were hungry, tired, thirsty, and now, to top it off, he was itchy.

"I've got it!" he exclaimed. "Powderpuff, go lean on the box like we did before. I'll make a run for it and jump against the wall. Maybe that will make it fall over."

When Spunky went to the far side of the box, Powderpuff trotted over to the cardboard wall, stood up on her hind legs and plastered her front paws against it. Over her shoulder, she watched her brother move his body on his weensy legs back and forth. Sheer determination was written all over his face. Then all of a sudden, WHAM! He flung his furry body against the wall and a half second later, the box toppled over.

The kittens were freed at last!

Their eyes were wide as they inspected the area where they'd been abandoned. But, unfortunately, there wasn't much to see because they were so short. All they could see was the sky and very tall grass in different shades of brown and green.

After they'd taken several loops around the box, they found a small path that led through the tall weeds.

"Well, I guess there's no time like the present," Powderpuff commented. She walked toward the trail, but stopped suddenly. Looking over her shoulder, she asked, "You guys coming, or what?"

"Are you sure we shouldn't wait here?" Trixie wondered. She looked about the strange terrain with uncertainty. She felt very small and she was worried that a weird creature might try to get her. It was just fine with her to wait in the box. She didn't understand why her brother and sister wanted to leave.

Plopping her little bottom firmly on the ground, she looked over at Powderpuff. "I don't want to go anywhere," she whimpered as the tears formed in her eyes and trickled slowly down her face.

Spunky walked over to her and licked her tiny tears. "Trixie, you're going to have to come on," he told her gently. "We can't survive out here any longer." He lifted her chin up so she would look into his earnest eyes. "Please," he pleaded, "please, come with us now."

Trixie's gaze flitted from Spunky to Powderpuff. Then, as if by magic, something inside told her that he was right. She stood up abruptly.

"I'm ready," she whispered bravely.

"Okay, but can you guys wait for just a minute?"

Flopping over on his back, he started rubbing his body all over the ground. He pushed and scooted and pushed and scooted until he had scratched his wee body so much, any thoughts he had flew out of his head. All he could think of was the incredibly wonderful feeling he was having as his itches went away.

After a minute or so, he rolled back over on his back, his two hind legs flat as a pancake, and stretched his front legs to their limits over his head. As he came back to reality, he slowly opened his eyes.

Powderpuff cleared her throat and tapped her little black paw. "Are you ready yet?" she asked impatiently.

He smiled crookedly up at her, then stood up and shook his skinny little body. A few tufts of fur fell to the ground. ""Wow!" he exclaimed. "That felt awesome. Nothing like a good scratch." He glanced at his sisters. "What are we waiting for? Let's go."

Powderpuff rolled her eyes, then laughed. As irritating as her brother could be sometimes, he was really funny.

Turning, she walked slowly toward the path that led to the mysterious lands, her uneasiness increasing with every step. All of a sudden, she stopped and turned around.

"Uhhhh, why don't you lead, Mr. He Man?" she said to Spunky. "It was your idea, anyway."

He trotted over and boldly stepped in front of her. "Hah! I'm not a fraidy-cat," he said haughtily. "You sissys go behind me. I'll be the leader."

He took an uncertain step forward as he looked up at the darkening sky. A rain storm was brewing and, already, a few rain drops had fallen, landing gently on his head.

"We'd better get moving before it starts raining harder," he told them. He motioned for his sisters to fall in behind him and, in spite of their fear of the unknown, the courageous kitties began their voyage to their destiny.

* * *

As they marched along, the three fell into an awkward kind of rhythm. Mindful not to talk too loud, they softly chanted a poem in unison.

"Hut, two, three, four. Hut, two, three, four. We are cats, and we love rats. Hut, two, three, four. Hut, two, three, four. We are cool, 'cause we don't drool. Hut, two, three, four —"

Suddenly, a flying object landed on Spunky's head.

"Hey! What's that?" he yelled. Looking up, his eyes crossed as he tried to focus on the creature. When his vision finally cleared, he saw a beautiful butterfly perched between his eyes, its wings fluttering.

He shook his head to get the butterfly off, but it wouldn't move. "Say, buddy, you better get lost," he shouted, trying in vain to swat it with his paw.

"You'd better look again," a musical voice answered softly. "Don't you know a female when you see one?"

"Oh, excuse me," he replied politely. "I didn't know."

Curious, Trixie trotted to where Spunky was

7

standing and looked up in fascination at the pretty butterfly.

"Hello there," she said. "What's your name?"

"I'm Priscilla." She flew to Trixie, fluttering above her.

"Hi, Priscilla." She giggled when the butterfly took several loops over her head. "My name's Trixie," she paused just before a sneeze racked her entire body. "And this is my brother Spunky, and my sister Powderpuff," she added, gesturing toward them.

"Pleased to make your acquaintance," Priscilla responded. She flew to a nearby twig, landing gracefully upon it. Her wings swayed gently back and forth while she studied the three scrawny kitties. "What are you three doing out here all by yourself?"

"We don't know, really," Powderpuff answered. "We were in this big box and then Spunky and I tipped it over, and we've been hiking for a long time and we're really hungry —"

She would have continued rambling if Spunky hadn't silenced her with a stern look. He walked beneath the twig Priscilla was perched on and looked up. "My sister sometimes goes on and on and on." He shook his head soulfully. "Sometimes she thinks she knows things, but she really doesn't. She's not very big, you know."

"Humph!" Powderpuff huffed. "I'm the same age as you."

She scampered to Spunky and playfully shoved him. Since there wasn't much to him but skin and bones, he fell over, landing on his side with a thud. He quickly stood up and marched over to her. Without warning, he pounced. Seconds later, she was pinned to the ground.

What skill, what mastery! He grinned at her struggling beneath his paws. Nothing like the thrill of victory! He glanced at Priscilla to see if she had seen his triumph. Then all of a sudden, he found himself flat on his back looking up into his sister's victorious face.

Powderpuff put her nose close to his. "You give?"

He frowned. "When's the last time you brushed your teeth?"

Hopping off of him, she giggled.

He quickly scrambled upright. "I'll get you next time."

"Excuse me," Priscilla interrupted. "If I'm not mistaken, you could use some food."

At the sound of the word that had dominated their thoughts for the last day and a half, the three starving kittens rushed to Priscilla and looked up at her eagerly.

"You know where we can get some food?" Trixie asked.

"I certainly do." Priscilla left her perch and fluttered above them. "You just follow me. I'll have you eating in no time at all."

Chapter Two
Lost and Found

It was strange how the world suddenly seemed brighter, the sky a little clearer, the air a little warmer — all because they had found someone who cared enough to help them in their troubles.

For some time, they had been jogging behind the fluttering butterfly and they were getting tired. But since Priscilla had promised them food, they pressed on, their empty tummies eagerly anticipating their reward.

Luckily, the grass wasn't as tall as before and Spunky could get a good look around. He was thankful that the humans had put them in a field near a neighborhood which meant that Priscilla was going to lead them right to a human's house. There they would find food, love, and a warm bed.

Just then, Priscilla came to a halt, landing with ease

on the ground in front of them.

"Okay, here's the plan. See that house over there, the one with the big van in front of it?" She pointed her wing toward a house across the street.

"This afternoon I saw the humans that live there put a big bowl of food out on the porch for their dog. The dog has already eaten, but I know there's lots left."

Powderpuff licked her lips in anticipation. "What do we do about crossing the street?" she wondered.

Spunky snorted. "We just run across, silly."

"But it's dangerous," Trixie protested.

"We'll be careful. Now, quit whining and come on. Don't you see our worries are over?" He grinned at her and playfully tugged on her whiskers.

"I'll fly across the street first and signal to you when it's clear," Priscilla said, lifting off as she spoke.

Trixie took a few steps after her. "How will we know?" she yelled.

"I'll whistle," she shouted back.

The three little kittens waited patiently on the side of the road until they saw Priscilla fly across the street and land on a big red stop sign. She looked up and down the street and then, a moment later, the wind carried the faint sound of her whistle.

"Let's go," Spunky signaled for his sisters to follow him before he raced across the street.

In no time, the three kittens were led by Priscilla to the back yard of the house where they found the dog's bowl of food on the patio beneath a pretty blue awning.

They hungrily gobbled up as much as their little tummies could handle. Little Trixie ate so fast, she got the hiccups. But that didn't stop her from eating. She'd just take a bite, then hiccup, then take another bite, then hiccup.

From her perch on the roof, Priscilla watched the three kitties and smiled. It was great to see them eating and getting some color in their little furry cheeks. Yet her happiness was short-lived when she remembered their desperate situation. What was she going to do about getting them a home? And food? A family?

Her thoughts were suddenly interrupted when Trixie shrieked with delight.

"Yummy! Boy, do I ever feel better." She lay on her back, then patted her happy stomach. Stretching as much as her tiny body would allow, she closed her sleepy eyes.

"I feel better, too," Powderpuff said as she flopped down next to her and yawned. "I think I'll just close my eyes for a minute —" her voice trailed off, her droopy eyes closed.

Not wanting to be left out, Spunky curled up next to them and closed his eyes. Within minutes, the rain began to fall steadily, the constant pitter patter on the awning lending a graceful hand to their much needed slumber.

Ever the dreamer, Spunky's mind was full of visions of cat toys, balls of string, and a warm, fluffy bed snuggled near a fireplace. Every time he slept, all he ever dreamed of was a home. Today was no different. Except this time, he dreamed of the family inside the house that would soon rescue them and make them part of their lives forever.

But Spunky and his sisters would have been sad if they'd known that while they slept, the humans who lived in the home were packing their belongings into the big van in front of the house. They'd bought a house in another city and the very next day, would be moving out.

Tomorrow, the kittens' new source for food would be gone!

* * *

By nightfall, they awoke feeling much, much better. A few more bites from the bowl of food took care of any remaining hunger and, soon, they were eager to explore and play, as kittens are known to do.

Powderpuff stood up and stretched; then her gaze swept the huge back yard, a ready field for her much anticipated match. She turned and looked over at Spunky. Padding softly, she walked to where he was lying and leaned over him, her soft whiskers tickling his tiny nose.

"Let's go wrestle," she challenged in a whisper. "I bet you I can pin you again."

Spunky reached up to tug on her ear. "You're on, Puffball. You just got lucky last time."

"Yippee!" Trixie squealed. "Can I be the referee?"

Spunky chuckled. "Sure, Trix. You're the referee. You tell me when I have her pinned."

Powderpuff's eyes narrowed. "Hah!" she snorted.

Not waiting for his response, she tore off for the middle of the yard. A millisecond later, she whirled around and crouched low to the ground, her tail swinging side to side like a pendulum, eager for the big event. She stared at her opponent greedily.

Across the lawn, Spunky sauntered toward her, his awkward paws pounding the grassy terrain. He searched his mind for a suitable plan of attack. Then it hit him. The mouse pounce technique! As he crept closer to her, his whiskers bristled forward, he tried to remember the right moves. Slowly. Slowly, he reminded himself. Don't rush it.

Suddenly, Powderpuff turned her body sideways and arched her back. This was the moment he was waiting for. The sign of weakness! As he prepared to pounce, he was interrupted by a sound from inside the house. Instantly, the three kittens looked up.

"What's going on?" Trixie whispered.

"I don't know," Spunky replied. "I think someone's coming."

"What do we do?" Powderpuff wondered.

Spunky narrowed his eyes as he thought for a moment. Then he took a quick look at his sisters and darted toward the back door. "Come on!" he shouted over his shoulder. "There's not much time."

Spunky and his sisters sprinted to the steps by the back door, barely making it in time before a little boy walked out. He was concentrating so much on the bowl of chocolate swirl ice cream he was eating, he didn't notice the three panting kitties sitting on their haunches on the bottom of the steps, trying to look as cute as possible.

And he also didn't notice Trixie's tail.

"Yowwww!" Trixie shrieked.

"Whhhhat?" screamed the boy as the bowl flew out of his hands, clattering to the cement.

Trixie squealed again before she whirled and took

14

off for the wood pile at the back of the yard, with Spunky and Powderpuff racing after her.

Having heard the shrieks and squeals from inside the house, Jake's mother appeared at the back screen door. It didn't take her but a second to notice the glob of ice cream on the sidewalk and the broken pieces of the bowl scattered about. Her son was standing in the middle of the mess, his chin a myriad of colors from the smeared ice cream that had escaped his spoon.

"Jake, what on earth is going on?"

"Mama! There's some kitties," he shouted, pointing to the wood pile. "They went over there."

"Don't move," she said quickly. "I don't want you to get cut from the glass." She turned around quickly and went inside the house to get a mop and broom.

As his mother cleaned up the broken glass, Jake anxiously shifted back and forth on his bare feet, his eyes glued to the wood pile. The clean up seemed to be taking forever and he was nervous. He felt so bad for stepping on the little one's tail. He wanted to apologize and make sure it was okay.

After his mother had finally said he could move, he ran to the back of the yard and plopped down on his hands and knees in front of the wood pile.

"Kitty, oh kitty cat," he said in a sing song voice. "Please, come out and talk to me. I didn't mean to hurt you. I didn't see you." His lower lip trembled. "I'm not going to cry," he said quietly. Glancing quickly over his shoulder, he made sure his big sister wasn't coming out of the house. She would probably tease him if she saw him crying. Besides, he thought, boys his age didn't cry. Why, next week he was going to be ten years old.

Finally the double digits!

Determinedly, he formed a fist and swiped it across his eyes. Leaning closer to the wood pile, he said softly, "I know you're in there, little kitties. Won't you come out?"

From between two logs, Trixie watched the boy and her heart filled with love. A split second later, she crawled out and sat before him. As she looked up, her golden eyes seemingly too big for her little round face, she blinked. And before Jake knew what to do, Powderpuff had appeared. He reached over and gently stroked her back. Her tail shot straight up and she started purring, the rumble vibrating loudly in her chest. Meanwhile, Trixie leaned forward to lick his hand.

When Spunky came out from behind the wood pile, he was happy to see his sisters had made a friend. Eagerly, he trotted to Jake and flopped down before him.

He rolled around and around on his back, looking up with delight at their rescuer.

Glancing over at his sisters, he grinned. It couldn't have worked out better. They were saved.

"Jake, Mom says it's time to come in," Jake's sister, Crystal, shouted from the back door.

He looked over his shoulder, lifted a finger to his lips, and motioned for her to come to him. Curious, Crystal ran toward him but stopped short when she saw the three kittens planted in front of her brother.

"Ohhh!" she squealed. "Kitties!"

"I found 'um," he said quietly. He looked up at Crystal anxiously. "I don't think they have a home. Do

16

you think Mom and Dad will let us keep them?"

Crystal leaned over, picked up Powderpuff, bringing her to her chest. She gently kissed the soft fur between her ears. "Let's go see." She turned and walked toward the house, with Powderpuff cradled gently in her arms.

Chapter Three
Spunky's Great Sacrifice

Jake quickly scooped up Trixie and Spunky and followed his sister across the yard. Even though the grip the little guy had on them was tight, the two kittens were careful not to squirm too much. This was their big opportunity and they weren't going to blow it.

Priscilla had been gone on a scouting mission and was just returning to check on the kittens when she saw Jake carting them into the house. She swooped over to them and fluttered above the boy's head.

"Trixie, Powderpuff — is he? Are they?" she sputtered. Finally, she managed to blurt, "Did you find a home?"

"We don't know yet," Spunky answered for them. "They're taking us in now to meet their parents."

"Good luck!" she shouted as the door opened. "I'll be waiting here for you."

"Cross your antennae!" he yelled just before the door slammed shut behind him.

Priscilla couldn't stand it. She had to see what was going on. Gracefully, she flew to the window and peered inside. The humans were standing in the kitchen and the three kittens were on the table. It looked to Priscilla as if the mom human had taken an instant liking to the kittens, but she was having some difficulty convincing her husband.

And inside the house, Spunky was getting nervous. It had started out so great. The little boy had wanted them from the start and the girl was crazy about Powderpuff. His gaze flitted from human to human as his stomach did summer circles. Talk about butterflies! He had so many butterflies in his stomach, he'd have to have a net to catch them all.

Suddenly, the human parents went out of the room and a hush fell over the small crowd as the two kids and the three kittens waited for their verdict. A couple of minutes later, the adults returned.

"Here's what we'll do," Jake's mom began. "Before we leave, we'll ask around the neighborhood to see if anyone is missing any kittens, though I seriously doubt anyone is. Seems to me as if they've been abandoned." She glanced at Jake and Crystal. "If no one calls, the kittens are yours."

She leaned over to stroke Trixie. "But kids," she added, "we can't have three kittens in our new house. Especially two girls and a male. You and Crystal can keep the two girls, but we'll have to take the boy kitten to the animal shelter." She looked at Jake earnestly. "You understand, don't you?"

19

A tear escaped and fell down his cheek as he gripped Spunky tightly to his chest. "What will they do to him in that shelter?"

"They'll find him a nice home," she responded gently.

His voice trembling, he said, "Won't he be sad leaving his sisters?"

"Not when he finds a new home." She reached over, ruffling his hair. "Look at that kitty, Jake." She pointed at Spunky. "He's a survivor. Don't you worry about him."

As Spunky listened to the conversation, his heart sagged. Although he was thrilled for his sisters, he was very sad he was going to be separated from them. Grief-stricken, he glanced at Trixie and Powderpuff. They weren't taking the news too well, either. He straightened his shoulders bravely and tried to look as if it hadn't bothered him. But it had. It had bothered him way down to the pit of his stomach.

What was going to happen to him now?

When the human family finally went to bed, the kittens were able to talk about the day's happenings. Of course, Trixie and Powderpuff immediately told Spunky they weren't going to leave him. Not under any circumstance.

Yet deep inside, Spunky knew he couldn't let them give up an opportunity like this one. It was a dream come true — two kids who could love them and give them a home. It would be dumb for them to shun their good fortune.

But Trixie and Powderpuff didn't see it that way and the three argued continuously into the wee hours of the night. At the end of their exhaustive discussion, they told Spunky in no uncertain terms they would not leave him.

About an hour later, as the sun began its rise in the eastern sky, Trixie and Powderpuff drifted off to sleep. That was the time Spunky made his decision. It was a decision that would be best for his sisters and would take a great deal of sacrifice on his part. He would leave. He would leave the only ones he had ever loved to venture out on his own.

With his heart bursting wide open, he took one last look at his sleeping sisters and left.

* * *

Several hours later, Trixie and Powderpuff awoke. As they stretched and prepared for their day, they noticed that Spunky was nowhere in sight.

"Where could he be?" Trixie asked, looking around frantically.

"I don't know," Powderpuff replied. "Unless — " She looked at her sister, her eyes filled with alarm. "You don't think he left, do you?"

"Oh, he couldn't have," she wailed.

Just then, Jake and Crystal walked into the kitchen laughing and giggling. At once, Crystal stooped over to pick up Powderpuff. She snuggled her nose to her, kissing her lightly on her tiny forehead.

"You're going to spoil that cat and then she won't be good for nothin'," he chided. He leaned over, scooping up Trixie. "See, I'm gonna train my cat to do tricks like those cats we saw on T.V.," he told her. His gaze swept the floor of the kitchen. "Say, where's the other kitty? You know, the one with the white hair under his chin?"

Crystal quickly looked under the table. Then she got down on her hands and knees and looked all around. With a worried frown, she looked up. "I think he's gone," she whispered.

"On no!" shrieked Jake. "We gotta tell Mom and Dad."

Once the search party was organized, the whole family, including Powderpuff and Trixie, searched all over the house for Spunky. They looked in the cabinets, in the garage, in the attic, everywhere. But they couldn't find him anywhere.

Spunky had vanished.

By noontime, the family had given up all hope of finding the lost kitten. Their search had revealed no clues and time was running out. They had to leave to meet the people who'd moved their furniture to their new house.

Jake's dad glanced at his watch for the umpteenth time, sighing heavily. "We can't wait any longer," he mumbled. He shot an exasperated glance toward his wife. "We weren't going to take that kitten with us, anyway."

"But where could he be?" Jake wailed. "What if he's hurt?"

"Jake, if he were hurt, we would have found him by now," his mom answered. "Don't worry, that kitty probably got out through Bootsie's doggie door and he's off rollicking and playing as we speak."

Jake's expression turned hopeful. "Do you really think so?"

"I really do," she answered. Reaching over, she tweaked his cheek, then turned him toward the house.

"Now go get your sister and let's load up your kittens. We're going to our new home."

Jake raced inside the house to get Crystal, and found her sitting on the floor in her empty bedroom watching Trixie and Powderpuff playing with one of Bootsie's toy balls. She looked up when he entered and he was surprised to see her face wet from tears.

"What 'sa matter, Chrissy?" The concern in his voice was obvious.

"Oh, I'm just a little nervous, you know, changing schools and friends and all that." She blew her nose loudly into her soaked tissue, then looked up at him. "Aren't you scared?" she asked softly.

He shrugged his shoulders. "I was sort of at first. I mean, I didn't like leavin' and all. But now, I've got a friend comin' with me." He pointed at his new kitty and grinned. "I just know everything's gonna be okay."

Crystal stood up, dusting off her pants as she rose. "You're right, little brother." She wiped her palm across her cheek to dry her tears, then leaned over to pick up Powderpuff. Kissing her gently on her head, she said, "I already have a friend, too."

He bent over and picked up Trixie. "I guess it's time for us to go."

She nodded, and as the two kids walked out of the room holding their kittens, Trixie and Powderpuff exchanged glances. Their destiny appeared to be decided. But they each wondered if they would ever see Spunky again.

When they were loaded into the human's van, they took a last look around. Suddenly, out of the corner of Trixie's eye, she saw a black tail flicking back and forth in the tall grass across the street. She jerked her head toward Powderpuff.

"Look! Over there," she mewed softly. She discreetly lifted her paw and pointed to the field.

"Where?" her sister whispered.

Just then, Jake's father rolled down the window to look outside as he backed the van out of the driveway. At the same time, Powderpuff leaped out of Crystal's arms and onto the top of the back seat. She clung to the vinyl with her claws, staring out the window, frantically trying to get a glimpse of her brother.

That's when Priscilla made an unexpected visit. She flew in through the open window, landing on the seat next to Powderpuff.

"Your brother has a message for you," she said breathlessly.

She was interrupted by Crystal's high-pitched squeal. "Mama!" she shrieked, "there's a bug in here."

"Calm down, Chrissy, it will leave in just a minute." She gently tapped her husband's shoulder. "Leave your window down so it will fly out. Her highness back there," she grinned over her shoulder at Crystal, "doesn't want that scary bug in here."

Crystal smiled sheepishly at her mother, then turned her gaze to Powderpuff. It was amazing. Her kitten wasn't even trying to play with the butterfly.

She watched as Priscilla lifted off the back seat to land on Powderpuff's forehead. Leaning over to whisper in her ear, she said, "I've got to make this fast, so listen up. Spunky wants you and Trixie to know that he will miss you very much. He left because he thought it best." She shifted to Powderpuff's nose to look directly into her eyes. Glancing quickly at Trixie, she continued, "And he said he will always love you."

Trixie left Jake's lap to leap up next to Powderpuff. She smiled tremulously at her.

"We're gonna miss him a whole bunch, too," she said softly.

Priscilla nodded solemnly. "I know you will," she replied gently. Looking around quickly, she said, "It's time for me to go. Good luck and God bless you."

As Priscilla started to fly away, Trixie halted her. "Wait. Please tell him we love him, too," she sniffed, "and tell him thank you. We understand what he did for us."

"I will," she answered. Fluttering over their heads, she waved farewell.

Powderpuff and Trixie watched Priscilla fly out the window toward the field where they knew their brother would be waiting.

Powderpuff sighed, then hopped off the top of the seat and onto Crystal's lap. She needed comfort from her new friend. She glanced at Trixie, who had also jumped down to lay on the seat next to Jake. The look the two kitties shared said it all. They would be forever grateful for the sacrifice their brother had made.

At that moment, Powderpuff closed her eyes and said a prayer that Spunky would be safe and that, one day, his dream would come true. He would find a family that would love and care for him, just as they had found.

Chapter Four
Hang Tough!

From his vantage point in the bushes, Spunky watched with sadness as the van drove away. At least he felt some relief because he was sure Priscilla had given Powderpuff and Trixie his message. Moments before, he had seen her fly into the van and he was waiting for her to return to tell him what they'd said.

Luckily, it didn't take long. As he watched the van drive farther down the street, he saw Priscilla fly out through the window and soar toward him. A minute or so later, she landed smoothly next to him.

"Whew! Was that ever a close call," she gasped, all the while trying to catch her breath. As she took in large gulps of air, Spunky stared in fascination at her willowy antennas wiggling in the breeze.

When it appeared to him that she was ready to talk, he barraged her with questions.

"What did they say? How were they doing? Did you tell them what I said?"

"Hold on a minute, Spunky. One question at a time," she told him gently. "This is what happened...."

Her wings swayed to and fro as she told Spunky about their conversation. When she got to the part where they'd said they loved him, he got sad all over again. Suddenly, he felt very lonely. Feeling much too sorry for himself, he lay down in the bushes and closed his eyes.

Priscilla could tell that Spunky had sunk into the doldrums. But she knew that if he were to survive, he had to snap out of it and get a better attitude. After all, he had plenty to offer a family. He just had to start thinking positively and it was up to her to make him.

Assuming a stern expression, she marched over and tapped him on his nose.

"Ehhh, hem," she said as she cleared her throat. The second his eyes opened, she glared up at him. "What are you doing?" she asked. "You're just lying around feeling sorry for yourself when you could be doing something about your situation."

"Like what?" he moaned. He closed his eyes again and rolled over on his back.

"Like what, he asks," Priscilla mumbled. She lifted off and flew tight circles above his head, creating such a breeze that he opened his eyes again and giggled.

She smiled at him. "That's better, Spunky. Now," she eyed him carefully as she landed once more beside him. "Let's see your walk."

"What do you mean, my walk?"

"I mean, I want to see your strut. You know, how you walk, so I can see if it measures up. You have to be able to stand out, my boy."

"Ohhhh, I see what you mean." Eager to please, he

27

stood up and walked around her in a large circle.

"What on earth is that?" she wailed. "You call that a strut?" She tapped an antenna on the ground. "Let's see it again. And this time, put a little umph into it."

He looked over at her, his eyes suddenly sad. "I don't think I feel like playing a game," he mumbled.

"Spunky, it's not a game," she said softly. "You have to learn how to behave like a cat. That way, if you ever find yourself in an animal shelter, you'll know how to act right."

"But I'll have you to help me."

"Maybe, maybe not." Her eyes softened as she looked toward the south. "Very soon I'm going to have to leave you. And when I do," she paused before she looked back into his golden eyes, "you're going to have to learn how to be on your own. And you know what?"

"What?"

"I know you can do it, because you've got what it takes."

"Are you sure?" he asked.

"Yes, I am. And what you don't know, I'm going to teach you. In no time you'll be ready to tame that jungle out there."

He stood up straight and grinned. "You're right. I'm going to make myself the bestest, most wonderful cat in the whole world and then no human will be able to resist me."

She winked at him. "That's the spirit, Spunky. Now let's get to work."

For the rest of the afternoon, Priscilla and Spunky worked very hard at trying to make him presentable.

She taught him how to walk, eat like a gentlecat, and clean his whiskers so they glimmered in the fading sunlight. By the end of the day, he was exhausted. And hungry.

"What are we going to eat?" he wanted to know.

"Well," she scratched an antenna across her forehead. "I think we're going to have to go in search of it." She looked at him, her eyes bright. "We're going to have to go farther into the neighborhood to see if any humans have left any food out for their pets."

"That sounds dangerous," he said quietly.

Priscilla nodded. "I know, but I don't think we have a choice." She pointed to his stomach. "You've got to keep up your strength, and that means you have to eat."

He straightened his shoulders as he glanced down the dark street. Since it was dusk, the street lamps had turned on and the flickering lights were casting eerie shadows on the ground, playing havoc with his imaginative mind.

What creatures loomed in those smoky shadows?

"Okay, I'm ready to go," he said courageously. He looked up at her, his big eyes so full of trust, Priscilla's heart melted. She knew right then she was going to do everything in her power to protect her furry friend — even if it meant she had to stay with him forever. She lifted off and sailed down the street. As he trailed slowly behind her, the different sounds of the creatures of the night began to fill the air. His eyes darted back and forth while he kept watch for scary beings.

After they'd traveled half way down the block, she floated to a stop.

"Okay, here's the plan," she began. "As I recall, there's a family that lives in that brick house over there." She pointed to a single-story home across the street. "They have a couple of dogs and they feed them outside." She raised her wings to take flight. "They have a fence you'll have to crawl under, but I think you can manage it."

"You going to lead?" he asked, trying to make his voice not tremble.

"Yes. Now stick close to me," she answered with a smile.

Spunky crossed the street, following closely behind Priscilla as she flew to the back yard of the house. After examining the length of the brown wooden fence, she found a hole that was big enough for him to wriggle under.

As he prepared to crawl through the hole, he whispered to her, "Do you see either of those dogs?"

"No," she whispered back. "It's all clear."

"Okay," he replied. "Here goes nothing."

When he arrived at the other side of the fence, he quickly glanced around the yard to make sure the dogs weren't around. Then he looked for the food. He grinned. Luckily, Priscilla had been right. It looked as if it was going to be smooth sailing all the way to the food bowls. He could see two plastic bowls right next to the house, underneath a water faucet spout.

Glorious, wonderful food was only a few steps away.

He trotted cautiously toward the house, mindful to look in all directions for the tail- waggers. Although he had never met a dog, he'd heard stories to convince him he needed to stay clear of them. Besides, all he wanted to do was get a little chow, maybe a little water, and then go to sleep. That was all.

As he began his approach, he could smell the savory chunks of beef stew in syrupy gravy. His mouth watered in anticipation. Two more steps. One. Two. Ahhhhh, sweet rewards. The culinary delight slid down his throat, oozing comfortably into the pit of his empty tummy.

After he'd packed in as much food as possible, he sat on his haunches to take stock of the mess to his coat. His survey was cut short, though, when he became aware of a strange new presence. He looked up, just as the two canines rounded the corner of the house.

"Yow-eeek!" he squawked. He looked around frantically for Priscilla, but he couldn't find her. What was he supposed to do?

Just at that moment, the dogs spied Spunky by their food bowls. It didn't take the smartest kid in class to figure out what he had done. The pip squeak had eaten almost all of their dinner.

Muffy, a tan colored mutt, stalked over to Spunky and glared down at him through thick mounds of hair that hung in front of her button eyes.

Mo, a much larger dog that looked all legs and mouth, growled at him, revealing rows of large, powerful teeth. "What do you think you're doing?" he snarled at Spunky.

Spunky froze. "I — I — I was ju — ju —" he stuttered. What was wrong with him? He couldn't seem to get any words out. He backed against the wall and stared up, up, up at the fierce creature, all the while trying to gather his courage.

Mo leaned even closer, his wet black nose only inches away from Spunky's face.

Then a wonderful thing happened. From behind the two dogs, Spunky heard a voice.

"Leave the kid alone."

Spunky quickly looked past Mo and was surprised to see a big, scruffy, yellow-haired cat. His fluffy tail was rigid and his green eyes were blazing as he stared fearlessly at the huge canine.

"Stay outta this, Stevie," Mo bellowed at him through clenched teeth. "The kid's gotta learn not to go browsin' in our territory." He jerked his head back around toward Spunky.

"I gotta mind to teach him a lesson or two."

Chapter Five
A Hero Named Stevie

"I said leave him alone," Stevie snarled, his heavy, well-muscled body, was tensed in anger. "Can't you see he's hungry?"

Muffy trotted over to Spunky to examine him. She was quick to notice that, although his tummy was bulging from his recent meal, he was really skinny. And his nose was running, which meant he probably had a cold. She looked uncertainly at Mo.

"Maybe Stevie's right. He doesn't look too good."

Spunky snorted. He was tired of being talked about as if he didn't have a mind of his own. "Hey, I can take care of myself," he said valiantly. "I don't need anybody."

"Yeah, I can see that. Helpin' yourself to our food isn't exactly taking care of yourself," Mo grumbled.

Muffy flicked her tail and sniffed. "Just get him out of here, Stevie. We don't want it getting around the neighborhood that we make a habit of feeding little kittens."

"You hear that kid?" Stevie told him gruffly. "It's better you hit the road and go back to your home."

Spunky glanced at the two dogs, then back to his rescuer. His head hung shamefully low as he spoke. "That's just it," he said quietly. "I don't have a home."

Stevie nodded his head in understanding. "All right, kid. You can come with me." He turned around and trotted toward the fence, his long bushy tail trailing on the ground behind him. Eager to be as far away as possible from the two canines, Spunky raced after him.

After they'd crawled through the hole in the fence, Stevie sat down to have a chat with the kitten. But he had no idea what he was going to do. Groaning inwardly, he scratched his head as he stared at Spunky. His solitary existence had no place for a kitten. He wrinkled his brow as he thought. Every cat he knew lived inside a human home and they were happy. And though he'd never been lucky enough to find a home — why couldn't he find the kid one? It would be a big project, but he figured he could do it. With just a little bit of luck....

He shook his head. "I hope I don't regret it," he mumbled. Raising his voice, he addressed Spunky with authority. "Kid, you and I need to talk."

"I realize I shouldn't have eaten their food," he replied innocently. "But I was just so hungry, and Priscilla, she's my friend, said it would be okay." He glanced around quickly. "I wonder where she is?"

"Oh, so you're not on your own after all." Stevie breathed a big sigh of relief. He was off the hook. The kid had someone else who was helping him. He stood up.

"Well, you ought to go find her. She's probably looking for you."

"I'm right here," Priscilla said as she sailed over, landing on a twig above the two.

Stevie stared at her in disbelief, then back at Spunky. "You're kidding, right?"

"Hi, Priscilla," Spunky smiled happily up at her. "Where 'ya been?"

Stevie, still in shock, practically shouted, "You mean to tell me this," he pointed at her, "this — this insect is the one who's taking care of you?"

Priscilla ruffled her wings. "I don't like your tone of voice, sir."

The look Stevie gave her was one of pure astonishment. "Oh, man. This is worse than I thought."

"I beg your pardon," Priscilla sniffed. "Have I offended you in some way?"

He brought one of his golden paws in front of his eyes and squeezed them shut. He had to be dreaming. He opened one eye back up and peered at the butterfly. Yep, she was still there, sitting primly on the twig as if she were queen of the world.

He glared at her. "So you're the half-wit that told the kid to go into a yard filled with yapping canines."

Spunky stepped protectively in front of her. "She didn't mean any harm, Stevie. She was just helping me find something to eat."

Priscilla nodded stiffly. "How dare you question me." She lifted off, fluttering above Spunky's head. "I have only done what I thought was best." She tilted her head proudly. "Come on, Spunky, if he doesn't want us around, we'll leave."

Spunky's gaze shifted back and forth from the butterfly to Stevie. Although the big cat had been gruff, for the first time in many, many days, Spunky felt relaxed and protected. It was a feeling he didn't want to go away.

"Wait a minute, Priscilla." He glanced uncertainly at Stevie. "Maybe we shouldn't leave just yet."

She quietly resumed her perch and waited.

Stevie shuddered. Not only was he going to have an anklebiter nipping at his heels, he was also going to have to entertain a butterfly. What was the world coming to?

Taking a deep breath, he faced the kitten. "Okay, kid, let's get a few things straight. See, I'm used to bein' on my own. Never had anybody trailing around after me. But I see you got yourself in a jam and I'm willin' to give you a hand. If," he paused, "if you listen to everything I say and don't question me, I can guarantee that it will be in your best interest." He shook out his fluffy coat. "Other than that, the rest we'll work out as we go along."

Spunky nodded solemnly. "I promise to listen and be good and do uh — everything you just said."

Priscilla's heart swelled as she listened. Powderpuff and Trixie were okay and now Spunky had found a good friend, willing to help. Her mission accomplished, she lifted her shoulders to take flight. "Young man," she said as she addressed Spunky. "I believe it's time for me to say goodbye."

"Goodbye?" he gulped. "Will I ever see you again?"

She blinked rapidly to prevent her tiny tears from falling. "You will see either me, or someone who looks like me. When you do, know in your heart that I will always be your friend."

Stevie walked over to Spunky and placed his big paw upon his shoulder. "She's right, you know. It's time for her to go."

Spunky sniffed. "I think I understand, Priscilla, but that doesn't make it any easier to say goodbye." He looked at her and smiled bravely. "You were very nice to me and my sisters. I'll never forget you."

"And I will never forget you," she said tenderly.

Lifting off, she fluttered above him. "Remember, think of me when summer is here," her voice trailed behind her as she flew gracefully out of sight.

Spunky sniffled, then glanced quickly at Stevie. He was afraid the tough cat might've noticed his eyes had gotten all watery. But Stevie was far too wise to make fun of him. It was good for Spunky to care for others. It showed he had a good heart.

Stevie stood up abruptly. "We gotta get goin', kid."

He stared up at him with wide eyes. "But where are we going?"

Flicking his wooly tail, he headed toward the field where Spunky and his sisters had been abandoned. "It's time you learned a thing or two," he said over his shoulder.

Spunky ran up to him. "What are we going to do first?"

"I'm going to teach you how to hunt for food," he replied.

"What kind of food?" he wondered.

"Mice. We're going to hunt for mice so you can learn

to survive on your own," Stevie explained patiently. "Stealing from dogs is a surefire way to get in big trouble."

Spunky nodded in agreement. "I remember."

"First thing you gotta learn is the approach," Stevie began. "And while you're stalking your prey, you have to be careful and be fully aware — and ready to deal with — any danger that comes along."

Spunky's stomach turned upside down. It didn't sound like fun chasing after mice just to eat them. In truth, he thought the little creatures with the skinny tails were funny. But he didn't tell Stevie. If Stevie was going to be nice enough to help him, he'd at least try to make an effort.

They crossed the street, plowing head first through the tall grass. By the time they arrived at the center of the field, Spunky was having a hard time catching his breath. Stevie was really fast.

Suddenly, Stevie stopped and crouched low to the ground. "Shhh!" he whispered. "Look over there." He pointed at a tubby, grey mouse scurrying along a path not far away from them.

"Wait until he gets closer," Stevie added excitedly as his large tail flicked anxiously behind him.

All of a sudden, Spunky felt awful. His stomach hurt and he felt dizzy. Just as Stevie prepared to pounce on the unsuspecting mouse, Spunky's stomach churned and he threw up.

Stevie stared at him. "What's the matter, kid?"

Spunky was so sick, he couldn't say a word. All he could do was lay on his back and grip his aching tummy. "Ohhhh!" he groaned.

Stevie took a long, hungry look at the mouse. It was so close that if he made any effort at all, the mouse would be his. He shook his head in disbelief. Anybody who knew him would never believe in a million years he could turn his back on such easy prey. But now he had responsibilities to the kid.

Unsure of what to do next, he walked over to Spunky and lay down next to him. If he wasn't better in the morning, the kid would need to go to the doctor. He wrinkled his forehead. Where was he going to find a doctor?

Spunky had barely enough strength to open his eyes and was happy to see Stevie laying on his stomach next to him, keeping watch. At that moment, he knew he would always be thankful to him.

These were Spunky's last thoughts before he drifted off to sleep.

Chapter Six
In a Pinch

Throughout the entire night, Stevie never left Spunky's side, in spite of the fact that he was getting very hungry. And as the morning hours began, he had time to reflect on how he was going to find Spunky a home. The little fella deserved better than living on the streets; it was way too hard a life. Spunky needed a home to call his own, with humans to love.

Stevie's thoughts were interrupted when he heard a loud roar. When he jumped up to see what was the cause of the commotion, Spunky woke up.

"Wh — what's wrong?" he asked sleepily.

Stevie's head jerked back and forth as he tried to locate the source of the sound. A second later, he saw a huge contraption plowing through the weeds toward them. Instant trouble! He had seen one before. He had seen what it could do to grass. It could grind up thick weeds and debris until there was nothing left but dust.

He whipped around. "Hurry!" he shouted before he tugged hard on Spunky's tail. "We gotta get outta here. Now!"

Grass went flying everywhere as the lawn mower roared over the grass they'd been lying on seconds before. More frightened than he'd ever been in his life, Spunky sprinted across the street after Stevie, but he forgot to look in both directions before he crossed.

He didn't see the large white van as it thundered down the road toward him.

Tires squealed as the van stopped.

Spunky halted in his tracks, unsure of which way to go. The big van had blocked one way and his paws were shaking so much, he couldn't get them to move any other way.

Suddenly, the driver of the van jumped out, making a bee line for Spunky. Just as he was bending down to pick him up, Stevie leaped, claws bared, onto the human.

"Ouch! Get off me!" the human shouted. He flailed his arms frantically as Stevie clamped his claws to the back of the man's jacket.

Stevie wouldn't let go. He knew the trouble Spunky was in. The man was the driver of the van that came through the neighborhood every other day to pick up stray cats and dogs. Stevie had never seen where the man took the animals, but he knew some of them never returned.

"I said get off me!" the man shouted again. He reached around his back, and this time, managed to get a good grip on the scuff of Stevie's neck.

"Geez, you got some sharp claws, big guy," he told Stevie as he pulled him off his back.

41

Holding him at arms length, he carted him toward the van. When the man arrived at the back of the van, he opened the rear door. Inside, there were six cages, most of them filled with other dogs and cats.

With Stevie still in his clutches, the man crawled into the back of the van, swung open the door to an empty cage, put him inside, and shut the door.

Stevie watched in horror as the man crawled back out of the van. For several breathless seconds, he waited to see if Spunky had been captured, too. Just as he was beginning to hope that the kitten might've escaped, the back door opened and the human appeared.

Spunky's petite body was squirming in the man's beefy hand as he opened the door of Stevie's cage to place him inside.

His gaze swept across the animals in the cages. "Don't you know you can get hurt living on the streets?" he asked.

A frightened silver and black cat with a green collar hissed at him as he moved passed her. Next to her, a stocky, black and tan dog barked and pawed the door of his cage.

"Everyone just calm down," the man told them before he crawled back out of the van.

A moment later, the door to the van was shut and the trapped animals were left alone.

Spunky looked at Stevie, his eyes wide with fear. "Where are we going? What's he going to do with us?"

He lifted his shoulders and shrugged without response. For the first time in his life, he had no answers.

Spunky glanced at the other trapped animals, then

back at Stevie. "I think I may know where he's taking us," he said quietly. "Priscilla told me about this place. It's a place where animals are taken that don't have a family."

The silver and black cat moved forward in her cage until her nose was pressed in between the wires. "But I've already got a family," she protested. "What about me?"

He shrugged his tiny shoulders. "I don't know. My friend didn't say."

Stevie hopped up suddenly. "Don't worry, Spunky. First chance we get, we'll escape."

"But what about the cages?" he asked.

"Hey, I've gotten out of worse pickles than this one," he encouraged.

Determined to distract Spunky as quickly as possible, he looked over at the silver and black cat in the cage closest to them.

"Say there, Ms. — uh — we haven't been properly introduced. This little guy is Spunky and," he puffed out his chest, "I'm Steve P, but everyone calls me Stevie."

"Nice to meet you, Spunky and Stevie. My name is Bonbon."

Stevie chuckled. "You mean, like the candy?"

She nodded.

"That's cute." He gestured toward her collar. "What about you? If you got a family, what are you doing here?"

She looked at the floor of the van, ridden with guilt. "I got out last night when my humans weren't looking.

43

See, normally, I stay inside. But I really wanted to go out and play. And, well, I wasn't thinking. I wandered too far away. Then right when I decided it was time to go back home, that man found me."

"Gee, if I had a home I'd never wander off," Spunky told her.

Humiliated, Bonbon looked away. She knew how fortunate she was to have a home. She should've known better.

"Yep. She's a lucky one," said Sappy, a black labrador who was in a cage at the front of the van.

"What do you mean?" Spunky asked as he quickly brought his hind leg over to scratch his ear.

Sappy pointed to her collar and tag. "That tag she's wearing means she's got identification. They'll probably call her humans as soon as we get to the shelter and tell them to come pick her up."

"How do you know?" the little kitten wondered.

Sappy perked his ears and snorted. "Them humans have picked me up a couple of times."

"What about your family?" Spunky asked.

"Awww, after a day or two, my owners come and get me."

Spunky wrinkled his forehead. "Why would you leave like that? What if someday they don't find you?"

"They will. They always do," he replied with a slight edge to his voice.

"I wouldn't risk it," Spunky said meaningfully. "If I had a family, I'd never, ever, ever leave. I'd be good and never run off, never cause trouble. I'd be a perfect angel."

"Hrmph!" Sappy grumbled. "It won't matter. I mean,

you can be good and humans will still be mean to you."

Stevie shook his head. "That's not what I've heard, or seen. There are a whole lot of really nice humans out there." He looked back at Spunky. "And we're going to find you some," he added.

Sappy chuckled at the twosome, lay down in his cage, and crossed his front paws. "Life ain't like that. You gotta fight to survive," he mumbled.

Stevie looked back at him. "Not always," he said softly.

Sappy bit his bottom lip, groaning inwardly. What the cat didn't understand was that he didn't want his humans to find him. But there was no way he was going to admit it to those goodie four paws. No sirree.

Conversation among the animals ceased as the van sped down the highway. And other sounds filled the cabin. Sounds that confused and frightened the tiny kitten. Clanging cages, whining tires, the loud roar of an engine followed by a shrill whistle. Sounds that were unidentifiable. Sounds that were unknown.

Suddenly, the van came to a halt and the motor was turned off. A second later, they heard footsteps approaching.

"Shhh! Everyone quiet," instructed Stevie. "He's coming."

The animals fell silent, each fearful of what their future would hold.

Would their humans find them?

Would they find a family?

Would they be loved?

Chapter Seven
Down in the Dumps

One by one, the humans who worked in the shelter carried the dogs and cats into the building, placing each one in a separate cage. The room that housed the cages was lit with a large light bulb that hung on a chain in the center of the ceiling. By the door, there was a big window cracked open.

When Spunky was carted inside, the human swung the door to the shelter wide open. A gust of wind followed them in, making the light bulb rock gently back and forth, causing funky shadows to dance along the caged walls.

Thankfully, Stevie was placed in the same cage as the little kitten and, as Spunky adjusted to his new surroundings, his stomach knotted painfully. He felt sick that Stevie had been captured. And for some reason, the itchiness that had disappeared for a while had returned in full force.

He sat down with a thud. What a mess he was in!

He looked at Stevie to see what he was thinking and was surprised when he grinned at him.

"Looks like we're in luck," he said slowly.

Spunky walked over to him eagerly. "What do you mean?" he whispered.

"If I can figure out a way to get outta this cage, we could escape through that window." Stevie pointed to the open window.

"Yippee!" Spunky shrieked. "We're saved!"

"I believe so. Now all we have to do is await the right timing."

Spunky grinned as he scratched his chin with his hind leg. "Whatever you say, Stevie."

"Listen, Spunky, you're going to have to learn to stand on your own four paws," he told him gruffly. "I'm not always going to be there for you."

Spunky nodded solemnly. "I know, you'll leave just like Priscilla did." He flopped down in the cage and looked up at the ceiling. "Everyone leaves," he said woefully.

"Don't feel bad, Spunky. Someday you're going to find the right home and all this," he made a sweeping gesture with his paw, "will be a distant memory."

Spunky stood up. "You're absolutely right. It's time I started thinking positively, just like Priscilla taught me." He glanced toward the door, then back at Stevie.

"Tell me what to do."

By nightfall, they had planned their escape, no detail left to chance. Now all they could do was sit and wait for morning.

The hours passed quickly for Spunky as Stevie told

him stories about when he was young. He was surprised to learn that Stevie was ten years old, which meant that his friend had the gift. His mother had spoken as if the gift was very rare. He didn't remember much of what she'd said. Something about nine lives. Spunky smiled to himself. He was sure that Stevie must have all nine lives packed into those ten years, and he was happy he'd had the good luck to know someone so special.

Closing his eyes, he listened to the gentle murmur of Stevie's voice. Before he knew it, he was drifting far away to dream land — where there were rolling hills of soft green grass, feathery clouds floating lazily across the sky, and a nice warm home filled with love.

A far cry from the place where the tiny kitten slept.

* * *

Morning arrived rudely, jerking him back to reality. He was quick to notice the several humans moving about the room, pouring servings of food into the cages.

His heart started beating rapidly in anticipation. This was the moment they'd been waiting for. He glanced at Stevie to make sure the plan would still go into effect and was pleased to see his nod of assurance.

If all went well, they would escape within minutes.

Spunky held his breath as the humans got closer and closer. He looked quickly at the door of the cage, then back at the humans.

Just a few more steps.

Finally, one of the humans reached over to unlock the latch.

"Now!" Stevie shouted before he pushed against the door and leapt to the floor. He looked up to see if Spunky had jumped, too, and saw a small mound of black flying in his direction at break neck speed.

Turning, he sprinted to the window and hopped to the ledge, with Spunky following right behind him. He nudged open the window and jumped to the ground.

Freedom at last!

He whirled around to tell Spunky which way to go, but he couldn't find him. Looking around frantically, he hoped against hope that the sinking feeling in his gut would go away.

It didn't.

When he heard the door to the animal shelter open, he darted behind one of two large trash cans.

"I'll see if I can see him," the girl who came through the door shouted to another human inside the room.

Stevie watched anxiously to see if he could get a look inside the shelter for Spunky. Then, he groaned. The girl was holding him in her hand, stroking him. He saw her scan the parking lot, then she eyed the two trash cans against the wall.

"Kitty, it's okay," she told Spunky as she nuzzled him with her nose.

Stevie came out from behind the trash can and slowly walked toward her. When he got within a few feet, he stopped and looked up at her questioningly. What was she going to do?

The human bent over and whispered, "Hi, there. Don't be afraid, Mr. Cat. I'm not going to hurt you."

Stevie backed away from her a few steps.

"What's the matter? Aren't you hungry?" She took a small step forward. "I want to help you," she said gently. "I want to find you a home."

Stevie hesitated for just a moment as he looked at her. Her use of the word "home" had stirred something inside of him he didn't understand. He looked at Spunky as he struggled to decide what to do.

Unaware of the turmoil Stevie was having, Spunky leaned forward and whispered, "Go on, Stevie. I'll be okay."

Stevie shifted back and forth on his paws. Finally, he asked, "Are you positive you'll be all right?"

As Spunky nodded slowly in her arms, Ashley looked down at him. Gathering him to her chest, she kissed his wet nose.

"You're just a little darling, you are," she cooed. She brought Spunky before her and looked into his eyes. Instantly, she noticed his nose was running. Next, she examined his ears.

"Ear mites," she muttered to herself. Stroking the base of his tail against the fur, she was quick to see the numerous fleas hounding his little body.

"Fleas, too. Kitty, you are a mess!" She scratched around his ear tenderly. "I bet you're going crazy itching, aren't you?"

In response, Spunky's purr rumbled in his chest.

"Well, don't you worry, Ashley's going to take good care of you." She rubbed his neck gently. "I'm studying to be a doctor and you can be my very first patient," she whispered in his ear.

Stevie sighed with relief. It looked like the kid was in good hands and could get the medical attention he needed. He grinned. Now he'd be free to work on finding the kid a home.

When the door to the shelter opened and another

human appeared, Stevie looked up at Spunky and winked. "Just leave it to me, kid," he said before he whipped around and darted out of sight.

Ashley frowned as she watched him run away. Once she was sure he wasn't coming back, she turned around and walked slowly toward the building.

"The big cat ran away," she told Justin as he followed her back inside.

He shook his head. "That's too bad."

She petted Spunky between his ears. "It's so frustrating sometimes. I mean, we could've found that cat a home. I hate him living on the streets." She looked at Justin with a strange expression. "I know this sounds weird, but I think he was getting ready to come to me, but he stopped all of a sudden."

He shrugged. "Hey, I learned a long time ago that you got something special goin' with animals." He motioned toward Spunky. "Where you going to put that kitten?"

"I don't know," she answered. "We need more room."

He clanged shut one of the cage doors and turned to her. "I know. We don't even have enough room for all the animals we have right now." His eyes swept the room full of caged dogs and cats. "I wish we could find a home for every animal that comes in here."

With Spunky still in her clutches, Ashley sat down on a stool in the corner. "I do, too," she said slowly. She lifted Spunky so that he was staring at her, eye to eye. "But in the meantime, let's just see what we can do for this little guy."

Spunky didn't have much time to wonder what she meant by that statement. The nice girl had taken him into a small room, rubbed some lotion in his ears, and scratched him all over. He was in such a state of happiness, he didn't realize what was in store for him.

But the sink full of water should have been a clue.

Ashley lifted him off the counter and strolled toward the sink, all the while cooing softly in his ear. "Okay, now little fella, this is going to be quite a shock, but you'll feel so much better when I'm through."

Before he knew what happened, his body was dunked into warm, sudsy water and Ashley was rubbing slimy, smelly stuff all over him. She scrubbed his ears and his stomach until his skin was sore. Warm water dribbled into his eyes and made them burn.

"Yowwwwwweeeeeee!" he squealed as loud as he could.

"Hush, now. You'll be okay in a minute."

He squirmed frantically, but it was no use. Ashley was much stronger than he was and she had decided he was going to be clean.

As quickly as the onslaught happened, it was over. She lifted him out of the water and onto a soft, fluffy towel. Gently, she rubbed the towel over him until most of the water was absorbed.

"Ahhh chew!" Spunky sneezed. He wriggled his body, unaccustomed to the feel of his fur being clean. Then, by instinct, he began to lick all over.

"There you go," Ashley said softly. "Don't you feel better?"

Spunky stopped licking to look up at her. As surprising as the bath was, he was even more surprised that he did, in fact, feel a whole lot better. Better than he had in days.

Ever so grateful, he leaned over and licked her hand.

Ashley picked him up and carried him toward the door. "We'll get you some food and then you'll be ready."

Spunky wrinkled his forehead. Ready for what? He'd had enough new experiences in the past few days to last a lifetime. But if being ready meant he could get out of the cages and find a home, he'd be ready all right.

He looked up at Ashley, grinning happily. Inside his head, though, he was shouting at the top of his little lungs.

"Get ready, world. Here I come."

Chapter Eight
A Diamond in the Rough

Stevie ran as fast as he could away from the animal shelter, through windy, dirty streets and across rough rocks and cracked cement, until finally, he came upon a big, green field of low-cut grass, scattered with huge pine trees. A large lake, with ducks and wild geese swimming lazily about, was in the center of the rolling field. Several homes, some with swing sets and bicycles in the back yards, were near the edge of the lake.

Stevie stared in amazement at the beauty around him. Never before had he seen such a place. It was so peaceful.

Far in the distance, a movement at the back of one of the houses caught his eye.

It was a beautiful Siamese cat!

Stevie watched anxiously as the small cat walked toward the field. When she got closer to him, he noticed how her face was the color of chocolate. He didn't think the elegant creature had seen him yet, so he stayed where he was and didn't move a muscle. There was no way he was going to chase away such a vision of beauty.

When she got to the sidewalk that circled the field, she stopped, flopped over, and rolled and rolled around on the ground, thoroughly enjoying the feel of the sunbaked cement.

He padded softly toward her, mindful not to make any noise. He just wanted to get a closer look. But all of a sudden, she leapt up and faced him, her tail bushed behind her, her eyes alert.

"Grrrrrr," she growled.

"Hold on there little lady," he told her quickly. "I didn't mean to startle you."

Her fur smoothed a little before she answered him. "Well, you did," she said pointedly.

"I was just —" He stopped talking suddenly as his jaw dropped.

Incredibly blue eyes focused on him intently. "What is it?" she asked a second later.

Stevie shook his head as if to clear it. "I ain't never seen no kitty as pretty as you."

She smiled slowly. "If you're wanting to flatter me, it's not working."

He grinned sheepishly at her, trying hard not to look like a goofball. "What's your name, little gal?" he finally managed to ask.

"That's close. My name is Little One."

"That name's perfect for you," he said as he sat down on the cement to stroke his golden whiskers.

"What's yours?" she asked politely.

"Stevie."

"Well, it's nice to meet you." She turned and started walking toward her house. "See you around."

"Wait a minute," he said, trotting after her. "Where are you going?"

"Back home."

He nodded. "Yeah. I saw you coming out of that house over there." He pointed toward her home.

"Uh huh," she responded.

He cleared his throat and licked his lips. "I wonder— "

She looked sharply at him. "What is it?" she interrupted.

His stomach gurgled loudly, filling the silence.

She giggled. "You must be hungry, Stevie."

"I couldn't have said it better myself," he said with a silly grin. "I'm too tuckered out to go lookin' for it," he added.

"You just come with me. I'll have you fixed up in no time at all," she assured him.

Stevie eagerly followed her across the soft green grass to the patio. When they arrived, she pointed at a big bowl of cat food. "Go ahead," she said. "Dig in."

He rushed over to the bowl and started eating. After several minutes, he stopped and glanced at her. She was patiently sitting at the edge of the patio, her tail swaying gently through the tentacles of green grass.

"You got quite a spread here, Little One," he commented between mouthfuls.

She sprawled out on the grass, resting her chin comfortably on one of her delicate front paws. "I have to say, I've been very fortunate." She motioned inside the house. "My humans have always taken good care of me. They're really nice." She sighed daintily. "I love them a lot."

"You got any other cat that lives with you?"

"Nope, just me."

He scratched his chin in contemplation before he said, "That's very interesting."

"Why do you say that?"

He stood up and walked over to stare inside a big window. "I was just thinking about someone."

"Who?"

"A young kitten named Spunky." He turned around to look at her. "He could use a home like this one."

Little One shook her head quickly. "Oh no, Stevie, hold on just a minute. I'm not letting a kitten move in here. All he'll do is chase me around the house, steal my cat toys, tear up stuff, take my favorite sleeping place, and just generally cause trouble." She smiled ruefully. "Shall I continue?"

Expelling a deep breath, he said, "I hear what you're saying, Little One, but let me tell you a story...."

An hour later, as the sun set behind the grove of trees in the distance, Stevie stood up and shook his coat. "That's all there is to it." He stared at the dusky shadows, deeply aware of the burden he was still carrying. He looked back at her.

Sighing, he said, "That's why I have to find the kid a home. He's all alone."

Little One bit her bottom lip uncertainly before she, too, sighed. "I hope I know what I'm doing, Stevie," she said quietly. "Let's figure out how to rescue Spunky and bring him here."

"You mean it?" he asked excitedly.

She nodded. "Yeah, I mean it. But we have a lot of work to do. After all, we have to find a way to get my humans to the animal shelter. That's going to be quite an undertaking."

He nodded somberly. "I know. I don't know how we're going to do that one."

Little One wrinkled her forehead. "At least you've come to the right place. You see, I'm a cat detective. I like to solve problems. It's what you'd call a hobby of mine."

She immediately turned and walked over to the rick of wood against the house, then leapt onto the window sill above. She lay down on the sill, then looked over at him through slanted lids. "Give me some time. I have to think."

* * *

For the rest of the evening and into the early morning hours, Little One considered Spunky's plight and rescue. When the solution finally formed in her head, she stood up suddenly, her delicate paws teetering momentarily on the window sill.

"I have it!" she said excitedly.

Stevie, who'd been sleeping soundly until Little One had shouted, awoke instantly. He trotted over to her and looked up.

"Yeah?"

"You say you were captured with Spunky yesterday?"

He nodded without speaking.

"So you know the schedule of the man who drives the van? I mean, you know when to expect him to drive through your neighborhood, right?"

His eyes opened wide. "You can't be thinking what I think you're thinking. Why, it would be insanity for a cat like you to go undercover. What if they didn't take you to the right shelter? What if —?"

Little One held up her little brown paw. "I've thought about that, but there's no use trying to talk me out of it. It's the only solution. The people from the shelter will read on my I.D. who my owners are. They'll call my humans and tell them to come pick me up," she said confidently. "And somehow I'll figure out how my humans will get Spunky, too," she added.

Stevie shook his head. "I don't like it," he replied grumpily. He looked back up at her.

"If I had known the way your pretty little head was thinking, I would've left last night." He scratched his chin. "I shouldn't have gotten you involved." Turning to leave, he said, "Don't worry, Little One, I'll figure out a way to help the kid."

She hopped off the window sill, landing gracefully beside him. "There is no other way," she told him stubbornly. "You know it and I know it."

He weighed Little One's words heavily before he finally spoke. "Well — actually, it is a good idea."

She smiled at him. "I thought you'd see it my way."

For just a second, she stared longingly inside her comfortable home. Then, without any more hesitation, she walked over to Stevie. "How much time do we have?"

"He'll be in my neighborhood tomorrow morning."

59

Little One expelled a deep breath. "I guess we'd better leave now then."

"Yep," he said brusquely. He stared at her openly, his admiration apparent. "You sure are brave, Little One," he told her before he turned abruptly and headed toward the field.

She smiled slightly and trotted after him, a determined look fixed on her cocoa colored face.

Chapter Nine
Bound and Determined

Racing after Stevie was much harder than Little One imagined. He was fit and strong and could race through whatever terrain they approached with ease. To the small cat, it seemed as if it had been at least ten hours since she'd left the safety of her home. But in reality, they'd been traveling for less than three.

Stevie suddenly made a quick turn, darting down another dark street. After several lengthy strides, he stopped unexpectedly, forcing Little One to also break her stride to stop beside him.

"This is my neighborhood," he said, looking around his territory with pride.

Before she spoke, Little One gratefully took a few deep breaths. "Nice place," she finally said breathlessly.

He flicked his bushy tail and glanced down the street. "It ain't too shabby."

"What do we do now?"

Stevie looked at the house to his left. "You hungry?"

She nodded.

As Stevie started to cross the street, he looked back over his shoulder. "Come on, I know where I can get you some food." He grinned crookedly at her. "It might not be up to the standard you're used to, but it's food just the same. Besides, you're going to need as much energy as possible to get through tomorrow," he added.

As if on cue, Little One's stomach growled as she walked slowly toward him. "I'd be grateful for whatever you can provide," she replied happily.

She followed him across the street to the back yard of a house, surrounded by a wood fence. He quickly scrambled through a small hole and disappeared from sight. A second later, he poked his nose back through.

"Your turn," he whispered.

With as much grace as possible, Little One crawled through the hole. Once on the other side, she glanced around the yard and instantly noticed a large dog bone to her right.

She shuddered and looked at Stevie, her brow furrowed. "Stevie, don't tell me we're in a dog's yard."

"Two," he answered before he laughed out loud. "But don't worry, Little One, I've known these two a long time. Just let me do all the talking."

The patter of dogs' paws on cement made her look up.

"Oh, my gosh!" she exclaimed once she saw Mo loping toward her.

Stevie quickly stepped in front of her, bracing himself for the approach of the Great Dane. After Mo stopped in front of them, Little One glimpsed around him and saw Muffy.

"Say, Stevie, I was wondering what happened to you," Mo's voice barreled into the darkness. "We heard you and that pip squeak got caught. How'd you get loose?"

"That's a long story," he replied. "Too long to go into now." He motioned toward Little One. "I'd like you to meet my beautiful friend Little One."

Muffy came around from behind Mo and smiled at her through her dangling bangs. "Nice to meet you, Little One." She glanced impatiently at Mo and tapped her front paw.

He frowned at her. "I'm getting to it, Muffy." He looked back at Stevie, clearing his throat before he spoke. "I'd like to apologize for my rude behavior the other night." He glanced down at the ground and pawed at an invisible object. "I shouldn't have scared the little tyke like that and —"

"I understand, Mo," Stevie interrupted. "The kid invaded your territory and you reacted. That's to be expected." He grinned at him. "I didn't think anything of it."

Mo heaved a big sigh. "Glad to hear it. Muffy and I have been pretty worried about you and the little guy. I was afraid I wouldn't have the opportunity to tell him I was sorry."

Muffy blew a stray clump of hair out of her eyes. She looked quickly behind Little One, then back at Stevie. "By the way, where is he?"

"He didn't make it," he told them slowly.

"What do you mean, he didn't make it?" she shrieked.

"No," he answered quickly, "he's okay. I mean, he's still at the shelter but he's still — you know, alive and all."

Muffy put a toast-colored paw across her chest. "Don't scare me like that again, Stevie. You almost gave me a heart attack." She sat down and breathed deeply to calm her beating heart.

Little One stepped forward. "I think it's very nice of you to worry about him. He must be very special."

She chuckled. "The kid's got nerve. Courage, too." She studied Little One closely. "You seem awfully interested in him. What's your racket?"

Little One wrinkled her brow. "What do you mean?"

Mo stood up to scratch his neck with his back hind leg. For a few seconds, the only sounds that could be heard were Mo's grunts. Once his itch was taken care of, he straightened up and eyed Little One warily. "She means, what's it to you? What's the kid mean to you?"

"She's going to give him a home, that's what," Stevie answered for her, gazing proudly at her.

Muffy's smile was toothy. "Wow! Is that ever good news." Her tail wiggled behind her, causing her small bottom to sway rhythmically.

"What can we do to help?" she asked.

"Yeah, what can we do?" Mo repeated.

Stevie gestured toward their food bowls. "The little gal could use some grub. I don't think she'd appreciate what I would normally have for dinner."

Mo chuckled, then glanced over at Muffy. "I don't have a problem sharing, do you?"

She shook her head vigorously. "Go right ahead. Eat as much as you want."

"Thank you a lot," Little One said graciously. She looked at Stevie. "Do you want some, too?"

"Don't mind if I do," he answered.

"It's all settled, then. Just go on over there," Muffy pointed to the food bowls, "and eat."

Thankful for the two dogs' generosity, Little One eagerly ran to their food bowls and began to eat.

And at that exact moment of time, far across the city, Spunky was huddled in his cage, feeling much too alone. For the first time in his short life, he had no one. No one to talk to. No one to seek advice from. No one to laugh with.

Ever since Stevie had escaped, Spunky had gotten an empty, achy feeling in his heart that wouldn't go away. And even when Ashley had been so nice to him, it was still there, pinning him down like a lump of clay.

Gloomy and dispirited, he expelled a deep sigh. Then he caught himself. No more self-pity. After all, tomorrow might be different. Maybe tomorrow he would find a new friend. He stared through the cage bars up at the ceiling and tried to recant his blessings, as Priscilla had told him to do if he ever were alone.

As the gusty wind whistled through the cracks in the building, causing multi pitched wails to assault his senses, Spunky closed his eyes and prayed.

"Dear God, I know you're up there. My mama told me all about you," he whispered.

He paused for a second before he continued, "I'd like it awfully much if you'd help me find a home and a family, so I can be loved."

As a tiny tear cascaded down his cheek, his thoughts flitted to his sisters. "And would you please take care of Trixie and Powderpuff?"

The tightness around his heart lessened just a little bit.

"Well, uh — thanks a lot." He opened his eyes, flopped over on his side, and closed them again. "Oh, and please watch over my friends Priscilla and Stevie, too," he added just as he nodded off to sleep.

* * *

Ashley arrived bright and early the next morning, bounding through the door of the shelter with youthful energy. "Hello, kitties and doggies," she said cheerfully to the room at large. Walking swiftly over to Spunky's cage, she flipped open the latch.

"And how are you doing, sweetie?" she asked as she reached into the cage and brought him to her chest, gently cradling him in her arms.

He looked up at her happily and purred.

With the gentleness of an experienced doctor, she looked into his ears and examined the base of his tail. She rubbed his neck with her long fingers, then scratched under his chin.

"You're probably feeling loads better today, aren't you?"

She carried him with her to Bonbon's cage. Swinging the door open, she expertly gripped the pretty cat with her free hand.

"Looks like you're sprung, kitty. Your parents are outside in the lobby waiting for you."

Bonbon let out a gleeful meow.

"I know," she answered. "You're ready to go home."

She whirled around and put Spunky back in his cage, clanging the cage door shut with one swift movement. "I'll be back in an hour or so, little fella. Don't worry."

Spunky watched with wide eyes as Ashley took

66

Bonbon toward the door. He meowed his goodbyes to her and sat down to await her return.

Ashley was right, he thought to himself. He did feel a whole lot better. He didn't itch any more and his nose had quit running. He glanced around the animal shelter and frowned. There wasn't much to play with, just a few toys, and he was tired of playing with them. What he really wanted to do was run and run and run.

He looked anxiously toward Sappy. In the night, he'd been awakened when the big dog had yelped in his sleep. It sounded to Spunky as if he were having a bad dream and the little kitten wished he could do something to help. But what could he do?

He lay down in the cage and fixed his eyes on the door, hoping that any minute Ashley would come back. Resting his chin on his paws, he closed his eyes. A little nap wouldn't hurt anything. He'd just catch a snooze while he waited.

Within a minute, he was snoring softly, his little body curled into a tight ball of fur.

Chapter Ten
Frisky and Fearless

Little One was nervously waiting in the tall grass beside Stevie when she heard the rumble of the van driving down the street.

"Now," Stevie shouted as he pushed her gently toward the street.

With incredible swiftness, Little One darted out of the grass into the direct vision of the van driver.

Mercifully, he slammed on his brakes and the van stopped. A second later, the driver opened the door and ran over to where she was huddled in the middle of the street.

From his vantage point, Stevie watched the man bend over to pick her up. And as the human carted her toward the back of the van, Stevie saw him study her I.D. tag.

"Good," Stevie said aloud. "Everything's going as planned."

He raced to the area behind the van to watch the man place Little One in a cage. As the door swung shut, he took a step out of the bushes to wave goodbye to her.

"Good luck," he whispered as he waved. "Till we meet again."

* * *

While the van rattled down the road, Little One surveyed her surroundings. Luckily, there was only one other animal in a cage and the dog had already made it quite clear he wanted to be left alone, which was just fine with Little One. It gave her plenty of opportunity to think.

She wondered what her human parents were doing at that moment. She frowned as she thought of how her human mom, Darla, would react to her being missing. Long ago, she'd seen her mom cry when she thought Little One had gotten lost. But she hadn't gotten lost. She'd just wandered around the neighborhood talking to some other cats that lived near her. Little One smiled shamefully as she thought of that night. She'd learned a valuable lesson. One she'd never forget. After she'd seen how worried her parents were, she had vowed never to worry them again.

She sat down in her cage and wrinkled her brow. That had been nine years ago. Since then, she'd never left the home except when Darla, Bill, or their son Noah walked with her out on the golf course.

She closed her eyes and sighed. She hoped they'd forgive her this time, too. It was an emergency, after all. The kid's future was at stake.

Suddenly, her thoughts were interrupted when the

van abruptly halted. A minute later, the door swung wide and the man crawled into the small opening. He opened the door to her cage and fixed a tight grip under her stomach.

"Come on, pretty kitty," he said softly. "Don't be scared. You won't be here very long." He carted her toward the white single story building. "We'll call your parents and they'll be here to get you quicker than you can say piggly wiggly on a stick."

Once they went through the door, Little One's eyes took a few seconds to adjust to the artificially lit room. At first, she didn't see the small black kitten hunched up in his cage. All of the other cages were full of other cats and dogs.

The man scanned the room, trying to find an empty cage. "I think you're going to have to share one," he told her when he stepped toward a cage filled with a tabby cat with grey eyes.

"Grrrrowl!" she snarled as the man started to place her inside the cage.

He brought her before him and looked at her, puzzled. "What's the matter, lady? Don't you like the big kitty?"

He glanced around the room and noticed Spunky quietly sitting in his cage.

"Maybe you'd rather be with a young 'un," he remarked. He moved swiftly over to the cage, opened the door, and placed her inside.

The cage door clanked shut as he turned around to leave.

Spunky stared at the intruder with wide eyes. She wasn't as big as the other cats he'd seen, more dainty and refined. He stood up slowly and circled her.

As he walked, her big blue eyes followed him, carefully assessing his movements. She was quick to notice that he hadn't snarled or hissed at her when she'd been placed inside his cage, which showed he had good temperament.

Next, she looked into his eyes. Nice eyes, she thought. Curious, yet eager to be accepted. Eager to be loved.

As if he knew he'd passed her inspection, he sat down and started cleaning his front paws.

She took a deep breath. "Hi, Spunky," she said quietly.

He immediately looked up. "How'd you know my name?"

"I know a friend of yours," she replied. "Stevie."

At once, his tiny body became alert. "You mean he's okay? You've seen him?"

Little One smiled patiently and nodded. "He's fine," she assured him.

He looked at her, grinning ear to ear. "He's my best friend."

"I know. He likes you a lot, too."

"Where'd you meet him?" he wondered.

"He came to my home yesterday, not long after he left here." Her gaze swept across the room. "It isn't too much fun being in these cages, is it?"

He flopped down and rolled over on his back. With practiced ease, he gripped the cage bars with his hind legs and pushed his body up, effectively scratching the entire length of his back.

When he was through, he stood up to face her.

"Awww, it's not so bad," he replied. "The humans are treating me real good. There's this one human named Ashley who's really nice. She gave me a bath and everything." He walked over to Little One, literally cramming his body under her nose. "See, don't I smell good?"

Little One obligingly sniffed his fur and nodded. "You smell wonderful," she answered, trying hard not to laugh. He was a funny kitten. Probably a laugh a minute, she thought. She closed her eyes and saw her peaceful existence in her home suddenly fly out the window.

Life with this kitten would never be the same.

And it was at that moment that Spunky spied the I.D. on her collar.

He pointed at the metal hanging around her neck. "You're a lucky one," he said wisely. "Your humans will come and get you."

He motioned toward the cage Bonbon had occupied earlier that morning that was already filled with a cute brown puppy. "There was a cat here this morning that had one of those tags." He walked over to the side of the cage and peered out wistfully. "Her humans picked her up. They took her home."

"That's what I wanted to talk to you about," she said quietly.

Their conversation was cut short when a family burst through the door of the shelter, led by Ashley. A sullen young boy, not more than eleven years of age, walked into the shelter. His striped shirt was soiled from the candy bar he'd just eaten and his hands were tucked stubbornly into his jeans.

He looked up at his mother and groaned. "I don't know why you keep taking me to these shelters, Mom. There's no way I'm ever going to replace —" his voice cracked as he thought of his dog that had recently died.

The boy's mother glanced at Ashley with worried eyes. She bent over and looked at her son. "We're not trying to replace him, Carl, we just thought you'd like to have another dog."

He swiped his arm across his nose and abruptly turned toward the door. "Come on, let's go."

The look she gave him was kind. "You're sure?"

"Sappy," Spunky whispered from his cage.

The dog looked over at him. He had been listening to the humans' conversation with rapt attention.

"Why don't you do something?" Spunky said quickly.

Sappy understood immediately. As the family started to walk out of the door, Sappy let out a string of high-pitched barks that made Carl turn around.

He walked slowly toward Sappy, his mouth open.

"Mom!" he yelled excitedly. "Look!" He pointed at Sappy's cage. "He looks just like Lucky!"

Sappy stood up and did wild circles inside the cage while he barked enthusiastically. When Carl got closer to his cage, he stopped and poked his nose through the cage.

"Careful!" his mother said quickly.

Carl looked over his shoulder at his mom. "He isn't going to hurt me. See?" Before his mom could stop him, he stuck his hand inside the cage and stroked Sappy's head. "He likes me."

Sappy moved his chin up and licked Carl's hand.

He looked at his mom eagerly. "Can we keep him?"

"Let's ask this nice lady a few questions, and we'll see," she said gently. She glanced at Ashley, then back at Sappy, her gaze studious. "He doesn't have a tag?" she asked her after a second or two.

Ashley shook her head. "Nope. And that's why on our books he's categorized as a stray. We've seen him every couple of months for the past year. He gets brought in because he's running loose," she continued. "His so-called owners take their sweet time picking him up, too."

Her eyes grew hard as she thought about the fresh welts she'd seen on Sappy's back the day before.

"Yesterday we finally got proof they abuse him." She leaned over and scratched between his floppy ears. Looking up, she said, "He won't be going back to those humans now."

Carl's mother walked over to Sappy's cage and crouched to the ground so she could get a good look at the dog's face.

"You want to come live with my son? You want to have a family?" she asked him before she reached inside the cage and gently stroked his back.

In response, Sappy barked. And if one looked close enough, they would have seen that he was smiling, a contented glow replacing the sadness in his eyes.

Spunky watched happily as the human family took the big labrador out of the cage, hooked a leash on him, and led him toward the door.

Just as he was being taken outside, he turned around and barked, "Thanks a lot, kid. You're all right in my book."

Chapter Eleven
An Answered Prayer

Little One had watched how Spunky had helped Sappy and she was impressed. Perhaps the kid had promise. Perhaps he could become an asset to her family. She smiled and walked over to the side of the cage where he was sitting staring forlornly at the door.

"We've got to talk," she said quietly.

Spunky turned his head toward her. "About what?"

"Your future."

"My future?" he huffed. "I got it all figured out. Ashley's going to take me home. She's been so nice and all," his voice drifted off.

Little One shook her head knowingly. "You can't be certain of that. She works here. She's a good human who cares a lot about animals, but it's her job to find you a home, not give you a home."

Spunky suddenly felt depressed. He lay down on his stomach, resting his head on one of his paws.

"I figured I was fooling myself," he said, much wiser

than his years. "But I've been working on ways to sell myself." Suddenly motivated, he hopped up and swaggered around the cage. "This is my walk," he said proudly.

Little One rolled her eyes toward Heaven. "Talk about jumping in with all four paws," she said under her breath.

"Spunky," she said firmly. "You're going home with me."

He stopped strutting and whipped his head around. "Are you serious? Do you mean it?"

She nodded. "Yes, I mean it. You're coming home with me to live with my family."

He suddenly felt very light-headed. The room swirled around him as he tried to catch his breath. Glowing eyes looked back at her. "You'll never regret it," he told her solemnly. "I'll be your friend for life."

Little One didn't know what the tyke meant by that, but she hoped it didn't mean a lifetime of chasing and stealing toys. But just the same, only time would tell what kind of adventures would be in store for the two of them.

Little One walked over to Spunky to face him. "We've still got to figure out a way to have my parents get you when they come to pick me up."

He sat down with a thud. "I didn't think of that." Looking up at her earnestly, he asked, "What do we do?"

"Leave it to me." She lay down next to him and put her thinking cap on.

All of a sudden, Spunky took off and started sprinting around the cage excitedly, his tiny body making circles around her.

She frowned at him. "You're going to make me dizzy."

"I'm just so fired up," he squealed as he ran past her. "I can't sit still."

Little One stood up to block his path as he started to whirl past her. "Let's play a game," she began. Luckily, she'd captured his attention by the word "game" and she was able to continue. "Let's say I own a big boat and you're a sea captain. Captain Spunky," she smiled as she spoke. "It's got a nice ring to it, don't you think?"

Spunky's head bobbed up and down eagerly. "Yeah, I like it a lot," he answered. "So what do sea captains do?" he wanted to know.

"Oh, they sail around the oceans while they navigate the ship. Let's see —," she hesitated for a moment. "They also perform rescue operations," she said a second later as her mind worked to invent an assignment that would keep his mind busy for a couple of hours.

"Who do they rescue?" he asked, his attention focused.

"Anyone who needs help," she answered simply. Her big blue eyes suddenly glowed. "I've got it. I've come up with your first assignment as a captain."

He hopped up and down on all four paws. "What is it? What is it?"

She smiled at him. His eagerness was a good sign. In fact, it was a very good sign. Her gaze turned thoughtful. Maybe he even had the makings of a detective. The tip of her dark brown tail moved back and forth as she considered that thought. She'd been wanting a partner for a long, long time.

77

Looking back at the little kitten planted in front of her, she said, "Let's say our boat is docked on a big island in the ocean and we've just found out about some animals that are stranded on a small desert island. But my boat is too big to sail to such a small island." She looked at him intently. "It's your job to figure out how we're going to get to the other island."

"Wow," he said as he digested her words. "That sounds hard."

She nodded slowly. "But I think you can do it. And you know why?"

"Why?" he asked as he looked at her, his eyes big and round.

"Because I think you've got what it takes," she replied.

He grinned crookedly at her. "That's the second time someone's told me that." He turned around and walked to the farthest corner of the cage and sat.

"Leave it to me," he said, repeating her earlier words. "I'll figure it out."

For several hours, Spunky was quiet as Little One planned his release. Every once in a while, she'd glanced at him while he sat huddled in the corner of the cage muttering to himself. She cocked her ear to listen to his ramblings and tried not to giggle. Then she smiled slightly. At least, he did what he was told. That was a very good sign.

When the door to the shelter swung open, Little One sensed her humans' arrival before she saw them.

For the entire day, Little One's human parents had been visiting shelters looking for her. Since they hadn't been home when the shelter had called, they didn't realize they were about to find her as they walked inside the door, their eyes anxious.

Darla gripped Bill's arm as she began a survey of the room full of caged animals. He reached over and tenderly patted her hand.

"We're going to find her, don't worry," he said softly.

She nodded and wiped a tear from the corner of her eye. "I know," she answered. Her eyes were bright when she looked up at him. "But if we don't, how are we going to break the news to Noah? He loves her as much as we do."

He expelled a deep breath. "I've thought about that, too," he replied a second later. "But let's just hope — "

Suddenly, he was interrupted by the loud howl of a cat. From her cage, Little One had howled. And not just any howl. This gal could howl louder than any cat in the whole world.

Instantly, they looked toward her.

"Bill!" she squealed. "There she is!"

They rushed over to her cage.

"Little One!" Darla cried happily. "We've been so worried about you."

Little One's big blue eyes widened as she stared happily at her owners. It was really great to see them.

No one noticed Ashley walk inside the shelter until she was standing before them. She leaned over and opened the cage door wide. "She's all yours."

Darla reached into the cage to get Little One. Hugging her tightly, she kissed one of her soft brown ears. "Come on, Little One, we're going home."

Ashley slammed the door shut, unaware that she'd shut it in Spunky's eager face.

As Darla carried Little One toward the door, Spunky's heart sank. She must not have figured out a way to save him. Soulful eyes filled with tears as he watched Little One being carted away.

But all of a sudden, Little One leaped out of Darla's arms and raced over to Spunky's cage. She stood on her hind legs and placed her front paws against the cage. Looking over her shoulder at her humans, she howled.

"What's going on?" Bill asked as he stared at her incredulously.

Darla looked quickly at him. "Do you think she wants that kitten to come with us?"

In response, Little One howled again.

Darla walked over to the cage and got down on her knees. She looked inside the cage at Spunky, then back at Little One.

"What's this, Little One? You want him to come home with us?"

Little One howled once more.

"Does he have a home?" Bill asked Ashley.

Ashley shook her head slowly and smiled as her heart warmed. It looked to her like her young charge was getting ready to find a home. "Nope," she answered. "He was abandoned."

"Well, he's got a home now," Bill told her. He walked over to the cage and opened it and in no time at all, Spunky leaped into his waiting arms.

"You're a spunky little fella, aren't you?" Bill said as he petted him.

"That's it, Bill! We'll call him Spunky," Darla practically shouted.

She hugged Little One tightly to her chest as she turned to walk out of the room and Spunky crawled onto Bill's shoulder, his claws gripping happily to him. A half-second later, the high-spirited foursome walked out of the shelter and into the warm afternoon air.

When the humans pulled into the driveway of their home, Spunky's eyes practically bugged out of his head. He could see miles and miles of grass and rolling hills of green. Looking up, he saw a sky dotted with white fluffy clouds.

Bill carried Spunky to the back yard and placed him gently on the ground. Darla followed closely behind him, carrying Little One. When she arrived at the patio, she bent over and put her right next to Spunky.

He shook his head as if to clear it and glanced at Little One, just to make sure he wasn't dreaming. Casually, he flopped over on his back to gaze up at the sky.

Then, he smiled. He had found his dream.

He was home at last.

Epilogue

Brimming with athletic energy, Captain Spunky stalked powerfully up to the podium to join Little One. Standing next to her was Stevie.

After receiving the nod from Little One, Stevie leaned over and carefully pinned a metal badge onto his collar. "Good going, kid," he said quietly as the group of cats standing before him cheered enthusiastically.

Suddenly, they grew quiet as Little One stepped up to the microphone. She held up one of her paws.

"Before we begin, I'd like to present a token of gratitude to our good friend, Stevie." She looked over at the golden cat beside her and smiled as she reached under the podium and pulled out a yellow collar with a green identification tag. As she leaned over to place it around his neck, she whispered, "It's about time you decided to find a family." She touched the tag around his neck. "This has your new human family's name and address on it."

He looked down at the shiny metal tag and grinned ear to ear. "Thanks, guys," he told them quietly. "Isn't it great that I live just up the street from you?" He looked over at Captain Spunky and winked. "This way I can still keep an eye on the kid."

Little One laughed out loud. Spunky had grown to be even bigger than Stevie and his black brawny shoulders towered several inches over his friend's.

"Now, back to the business at hand." Raising her voice slightly, Little One addressed the crowd before them. "This is a great day for my best friend, Captain Spunky," she began. She looked over at him and smiled broadly.

"The day I met him," she placed her front paw over her heart, "will stay etched in my mind forever. And I wasn't sure what life would be like when he came to live with my, I mean, our family."

She took a deep breath to keep from becoming too emotional and then let out a stream of giggles. "It took a few years to adjust to the kid but I'd say he turned out to be a great addition to my life, to my family — " Her voice got louder.

"And to the cats of America!" she yelled.

"Ya! Ya for Captain Spunky!" his crowd of friends responded.

Little One waited until they had calmed down to finish her speech. She leaned over and gave him a kiss on his cheek. Straightening, she looked back over the crowd, her eyes shining intently. "Together, Captain Spunky and I promise to fight for what's right in the world. We promise to help those in need. And we promise to right what is wrong," she shouted.

Once again, the cheers erupted.

Captain Spunky took a deep breath and glanced at Little One and Stevie. With great pride, he held up his paw to take his oath.

"I will serve the Cat Detectives of America with integrity and honor. And," he grinned at Little One. "I will always protect and care for others, no matter how big — no matter how small."

Little One wiped a tear from her eyes while she listened. Yep, the kid had come a long way. But even from the very beginning, from the very start, he'd shown her he was special. And now he was ready to share with the world his talents and skills.

As a beautiful butterfly flew over their heads, Little One sighed happily.

It was time to begin their adventures together.

THE END

Captain Spunky's Cat Laughs and Riddles

What do Captain Spunky and Little One like to put on their hamburger?

What do Captain Spunky and Little One do when they get super, duper tired?

What's Captain Spunky and Little One's favorite car?

What's Captain Spunky and Little One's favorite insect to play with?

What do Captain Spunky and Little One like to read?

What did Captain Spunky say when he ran the 50-yard dash?

See answers on last page!

Cat Detectives of America
News Flash!

Dear Cat Friends:

Guess what? The Cat Detectives of America has news for you! They're looking for kids, cat lovers, and animal lovers, who want to help and protect others, no matter how big — no matter how small.

They also want to make sure you are a person who always wants to do what's right. If you think you can meet these requirements, then we'll make you a member of our purrrrrrfect Cat Detectives of America club.

All you have to do is send your name and address (print, please, no cursive), and a check or money order in the amount of $12.95 (includes postage and handling), made payable to: Cat Detectives of America Club, at the following address: Cat Detectives, Attn: Club Membership, P.O. Box 1077, Oklahoma City, Oklahoma 73101. Or, you can visit our really cool web site at: www.catdetectives.com and join our club on line.

Then, in a couple of weeks (quicker than you can say piggly wiggly on a stick), you'll get an official certificate saying you're a member of the Cat Detectives of America club; stickers of Little One and Captain Spunky; and a really neat Cat Detective's badge that will tell all your friends that we think you are special.

And then for one whole year, you'll also receive a quarterly newsletter (that's four a year) that will tell you all about the different adventures that Little One and Captain Spunky are having around the world.

Also, we'll send you a coupon for .50 cents off your online purchase of the next release in the Cat Detectives' series, Tale of Three Amigos.

We really look forward to hearing from you. And thanks for being our friend.

Until next time....

Little One and Captain Spunky

WORDFIND

```
A  K  W  R  E  S  T  L  E  J  X  U  W  W  O  V
B  N  L  T  K  S  N  T  A  C  Y  T  T  I  K  I
U  D  O  A  O  W  E  H  E  L  P  T  R  O  R  D
T  M  A  X  B  U  Y  M  W  E  H  T  E  D  L  E
T  T  T  I  K  R  U  C  A  K  R  Y  W  Y  C  N
E  T  R  I  X  M  A  O  R  I  Q  I  O  E  A  T
R  R  W  N  A  E  I  D  X  C  S  K  M  A  T  I
F  S  T  E  V  I  E  I  O  C  K  E  N  H  X  F
L  V  R  R  P  Q  E  T  U  R  L  S  W  A  R  I
Y  D  B  A  B  Y  S  P  U  N  K  Y  A  I  Z  C
I  U  X  L  L  A  B  F  F  U  P  O  L  S  Z  A
X  I  D  E  N  T  I  F  I  C  A  T  I  O  N  N
```

Cat Detectives: See if you can find these words:

Instructions: words are forwards, backwards, up or down, and diagonal. Good luck!

BUTTERFLY	TRIXIE
DREAM	PUFFBALL
STEVIE	LAWN MOWER
BABY SPUNKY	SIAMESE
LABRADOR	IDENTIFICATION
WRESTLE	KITTY CAT

Answers to Captain Spunky's cat laughs and riddles: catsup, catnap, cadillac, caterpillar, catalogue, can't cats me!

(riddles by Noah Zuhdi!)